Stories of King Arthur

by

HERBERT WILLIAMS

Illustrations by Jonathan Ward

JOHN JONES

STORIES OF KING ARTHUR

This edition first published May 1990
Reprinted September 1994
New edition March 1997
Reprinted March 1998

K.

Cover typography by Elgan Davies
Cover illustration by Wendy Hesse

ISBN 1 871083 50 8

Printed by Cambrian Printers, Aberystwyth

Published by
JOHN JONES PUBLISHING LTD.
Clwydfro Business Centre
Ruthin
North Wales
LL15 1NJ

Contents

For my dear grandchildren
Darren, Andrew, Rachael and Joey

My friend and publisher John Idris Jones suggested that I write these stories after hearing some Arthurian tales I wrote for BBC Wales schools broadcasts. My thanks to Gwynn C. Griffith, who commissioned those scripts.

Merlin's Grandfather

The Two Dragons

Long, long ago there was a little boy called Merlin. His mother was a princess, but he never knew her because on the very day that he was born she went away from home to live in an abbey. Don't ask me why, but remember this was a long time ago, and people did strange things – even stranger things, perhaps, than they do today.

Now, you may think that poor Merlin had a very bad start in life, because not only did his mother leave him like that, but he never knew his father at all. Whenever he asked about him, no-one would say a word. Merlin thought it very peculiar, and it did make him feel a bit sad.

The good thing is that Merlin had a very kind grandfather, who brought him up as his own son. They lived in a palace, because Merlin's grandfather was a king! He ruled over that part of South Wales now known as Dyfed, and his palace was in the town of Carmarthen. Perhaps you've been there, but I'm afraid you won't find any trace of the palace any longer – it vanished long ago.

Now, when Merlin was still a small boy he found out that his grandfather was very special indeed. Not only was he a king, he was a magician as well! That's to say, he could see into the future and look back into the past. He could read people's minds, too – he knew just what they were thinking, even though they didn't say a word.

One day some soldiers came to the palace. They were

very smart and wore tunics with red dragons on them. 'King Vortigern wants to see you,' they told Merlin. 'You have to come right away!'

Merlin was quite a big boy by this time, about nine or ten, and he knew that Vortigern was even more powerful than his grandfather – in fact, he was the King of All Britain.

'Why does he want me?' asked Merlin.

'Because he needs your help,' said the soldiers. 'We can't say any more than that. King Vortigern will tell you himself, when you get there.'

Merlin didn't want to go, because he knew that King Vortigern lived very far away in North Wales. In fact, the king was building a new castle just below Snowdon, the highest mountain in Wales. Remember, this was a long time before such things as cars and trains were invented, and the only way to go anywhere was on horseback.

'Do I really have to go?' Merlin asked.

'Of course you must,' his grandfather replied. 'When King Vortigern gives a command, we must all obey. But I want you to remember something I haven't told you before. When I die, all my magical powers will come to you!'

'Please don't talk about dying,' said Merlin. 'I want you to live for ever!'

But the old man only gave a sad little shake of the head, and turned away quickly.

The very next day, the journey began. And what a journey it was! They had to cross steep hills and many rivers, and there were times when poor Merlin wondered if they would ever get there. But at last they reached Dinas Emrys, where Vortigern was building his castle. And Merlin still didn't know why they had taken him all that way.

Journey to Vortigen's Castle

King Vortigern was a tall man with bright blue eyes and a white beard. He had a sword at his side and a way of looking at people as if he didn't trust them.

When he smiled at Merlin, Merlin didn't trust *him* either! It's because he smiled as if he didn't mean it – the smile disguised what he was really thinking.

'Welcome to Dinas Emrys,' said King Vortigern. 'Did you have a safe journey?'

'Yes, thank you,' replied Merlin. 'But sir, I must confess that I didn't want to come. I wanted to stay at home with my grandfather.'

At that, the king looked very serious. 'My boy,' he said quietly, 'we cannot always have what we want in life.

7

Come.' And he took Merlin to the place where the workmen were building his castle.

'These walls keep falling down, even though they are built on solid rock,' said King Vortigern. 'I want you to tell me why.'

Merlin felt a little frightened, because he wondered what would happen if he gave the king a wrong answer. 'Why do you ask me that question, sir,' he said, 'when you have so many wise men in your court?'

'Even the wisest man,' said the king, 'is not the equal of Merlin. Now, close your eyes and tell me what you see.'

Merlin, wondering at the king's words, closed his eyes. 'I see a cave,' he said. 'It is right under the castle. Only a thin crust of rock covers the top of the cave – that is why the walls keep tumbling down!'

'Good boy,' said the king. 'What else do you see?'

'I see a deep pool in the cave,' said Merlin, 'with two hollow stones at the bottom. There is a dragon sleeping in each stone. One dragon is red, the other white. You must drain the pool and then fill in the cave, to give your castle firm foundations.'

King Vortigern's face had gone deathly white. 'So be it,' he said. And he gave the command for the pool to be drained.

When the pool was empty, a rumbling sound was heard from the stones. Then a dragon burst out of each – one red, the other white, just as Merlin had said.

Dragon Fight

And with fierce cries, the dragons began fighting each other.

King Vortigern clutched hold of Merlin. 'Which dragon will win?' he asked. 'The red or the white?'

'The white,' answered Merlin – for somehow he knew this, without thinking.

The king moaned.

Suddenly the white dragon gave a triumphant roar. The red dragon lay dead at its feet.

King Vortigern covered his face with his hands.

The white dragon raised its great wings and flew away.

It was only much later that Merlin realised what all this meant.

The red dragon stood for Vortigern, and the white dragon for two princes whose father he had murdered. Their names were Aurelius and Uther.

They were only children when their father was murdered, so they had been taken across the sea to Brittany to grow up in safety. Now they were old enough to return with an army, to avenge their father's death.

They defeated King Vortigern in battle and killed him. So the fight between the red dragon and the white dragon was a sign of things to come.

And how had Merlin known about the underground cave and the dragons?

Well, I fear his grandfather was dead by then – so just as the old man had predicted, all his magical powers had passed on to Merlin!

The Sword in the Stone

After King Vortigern's death, Aurelius – who was older than his brother Uther – became King of All Britain. I'm afraid, though, that Britain was not a happy country at that time. There were lots of civil wars, which means that people from one part of the country would fight people from another part. Only a very strong king could keep order. Aurelius did his best, but it wasn't really good enough.

Aurelius had been king for only a few years when he was poisoned by one of his enemies. So Uther became king. He called himself Uther Pendragon, but instead

Uther's Flag

of having a white dragon on his flag, he now had a golden dragon.

Uther looked every inch a king. He was tall and strong

11

and good-looking. He believed in treating people fairly, but his one fault was that he had a quick temper. When he was a boy he was always getting into arguments and fights, because he lost his temper so easily! He tried to keep calm when he became king, but didn't always succeed.

When King Uther fell in love with a beautiful woman called Igraine, he naturally wanted to marry her. That wasn't possible, however, because she was married to someone else – the Duke of Tintagel in Cornwall.

Uther was so unhappy that he sent for Merlin, who was grown up by now. 'I'm in love with Igraine,' he said. 'All I want is to be with her. Can you help me?'

Merlin looked very serious. Remember, he could see into the future.

'You will be married to Igraine before long,' he said, 'and she will have a baby boy. But you must make me a solemn promise – that as soon as he is born you must place him in my care. If he is brought up in your court he will be in great danger.'

King Uther was so glad to know he would soon be married to Igraine that he made the promise without thinking twice about it.

Soon after this, the Duke of Tintagel was killed in battle. Igraine was not as sad about this as she should have been, because she had been secretly in love with King Uther for a long time.

There came the day when Uther asked Igraine to

marry him. Of course, she agreed – and when they put the crown on her head, the jewels in it sparkled like a thousand stars.

She had a baby boy, just as Merlin had predicted, and they decided to call him Arthur.

She wept when he was taken from her, but she knew that Uther's promise to Merlin had to be kept.

'It is all for the best,' Uther told her. 'We have Merlin's word for it that our son will be in great danger if he remains with us here.'

So little Arthur, the bonniest of babies, was taken

Arthur as a baby

away from King Uther's court. Merlin place him in the care of Sir Ector, a knight who lived near the town of Carmarthen. Sir Ector was a good man and his wife was a good woman, and although they already had a son of their own they treated Arthur as if he were their own flesh and blood.

Their son's name was Kay, and he was four years older than Arthur. Luckily he wasn't a bit jealous of the newcomer to the family – he'd always wanted a little brother, and now he had one! So the boys grew up together, in the lovely countryside of Dyfed. They fished in the river Tywi, and when they were old enough they rode on horseback to Llandeilo and Kidwelly and even as far as the tiny fishing village destined to grow into the seaside resort of Tenby. They loved to be out of doors and Kay looked forward to the time when he would be old enough to be dubbed a knight, like his father – that meant he would be *Sir* Kay. But he wasn't sure if Arthur would ever be a knight, as he knew that his father and mother weren't really Arthur's parents. If he had known that Arthur was a true-born prince, what a shock he would have had! But even his father, Sir Ector, didn't know this – Merlin had thought it best not to tell him.

On the whole, in spite of his outbursts of temper, Uther ruled his kingdom wisely, so there was much sadness in the land when it became known that he was ill. It was, I'm afraid, a long illness, and when he died people said things like, 'The poor king had suffered enough. At least he will be out of his agony now.' But the country was in a terrible state! You see, hardly anyone knew who the rightful king should be, now that Uther was dead. Of course, Merlin knew that Arthur was the heir to the throne, and so did Queen Igraine, but Merlin told Igraine not to say a word about it. 'Arthur has to prove himself,' he said.

When Arthur was fifteen years old, Merlin invited all the important people in the realm to London, where they found a big stone in a churchyard. There was a sword stuck in the stone, with a message beside it saying, 'Whoever pulls this sword out is the rightful King of Britain.'

You can imagine what happened next – all the men who wanted to be king tried to pull the sword out! But no-one could budge it – even the strongest men failed.

Then a tournament was arranged. All the knights, who were the bravest people in the land, put on their shining armour and mounted their horses. Their horses were tall and strong, and when the knights sat on them their helmets seemed to be touching the sky.

The knights had bright plumes of feathers in their helmets, and they carried lances – long sticks with sharp points at the end. The idea was to knock one another off their horses with their lances, as they rode full gallop – what a sight that was!

It was agreed that when the tournament was over, all the knights should once more try to pull the sword from the stone. There was great excitement over this – everyone wanted to know who the rightful King of Britain was.

Now one of the knights taking part in the tournament was none other than Kay – he was Sir Kay now. Arthur was very proud of him, and they rode to the tournament field side by side on their horses. But Kay suddenly realised he had forgotten his sword!

'I must have left it behind at the place where we stayed last night,' he told Arthur. 'Do you mind going back to fetch it for me?'

'Not in the least,' said Arthur – he would do anything for his brother.

When he reached the inn where they had spent the night, however, he could not get in because all the doors were locked – everyone had gone to the tournament.

Arthur was very upset, until he remembered seeing something strange on his way to the inn – a sword stuck fast in a big stone.

'It doesn't seem to belong to anyone,' he said to himself. 'Surely no-one would mind if Kay borrowed it for the tournament?'

So he rode back to the stone, as quickly as he could. He got down from his horse and gave the sword a mighty tug – but to his surprise it came out without any trouble at all.

When Arthur handed the sword to his brother, Kay gave him a strange look and said, 'Where did you get this?' For Kay recognised the sword.

Arthur told him how he had pulled it out of the stone.

'Didn't you read the message?' asked Kay.

'What message?' asked Arthur. For to tell you the truth, he'd been in too much of a hurry to read anything.

Then Kay did a very wicked thing. He went to his

Arthur drawing sword

father, Sir Ector, and said 'See what I have here. Doesn't this make me the rightful King of Britain?'

Sir Ector looked hard at Kay. 'Tell me the truth, son,' he said quietly. 'How did this sword come into your hands?'

Kay blushed. He couldn't tell his father a lie. 'Arthur gave it to me,' he admitted.

Sir Ector mounted his horse right away, and he and Kay rode back to Arthur. 'Come with us,' said Sir Ector, and the three of them rode to the stone.

'Now,' said Sir Ector to Arthur, 'put the sword back in the stone.'

Arthur did as he was told, and the sword stuck in there fast.

'Right,' said Sir Ector to Kay. 'Let me see you pull it out.'

Kay pulled and pulled with all his might, but the sword would not budge an inch.

'That's enough,' said Sir Ector, and turned to Arthur. 'Now you try.'

Arthur stepped forward, and drew the sword out as easily as drawing a knife from butter.

Sir Ector took a deep breath, and knelt at his feet.

'Why are you doing that?' asked Arthur in amazement.

'Because you are the true King of Britain,' Sir Ector replied.

When the tournament was over, all the knights tried once more to pull the sword from the stone. Not one inch did it budge.

Then, with everyone watching, Arthur drew out the sword and held it aloft.

The knights went on their knees and paid homage to Arthur.

And that is how Arthur became King of All Britain.

The First Britons

Arthur knew he had a lot to learn, because he was so young when he became king. He had lots of people to give him advice, but the person he relied on most was Merlin.

'You're like a father to me,' said Arthur. 'I don't know what I'd do without you.'

Merlin telling Arthur stories

What Arthur liked best was going out riding with Merlin. The magician told Arthur things nobody had ever told him before. He explained how the island of Britain had once been joined to France, until the sea washed over the lowlands to form the channel that now divides us from the Continent. And he also had a strange tale to tell of a lost land beneath Cardigan Bay, a land known as Cantre'r Gwaelod. The waters had rushed over this too, but if you listen carefully as you walk the cliffs between Aberystwyth and Borth you can sometimes hear the bells of the drowned villages tolling far beneath the waves.

But the story Arthur liked best of all took him back to the very first days of his kingdom.

'Once upon a time,' said Merlin, 'there were no people living in Britain at all. There were only wild animals like wolves and bears, and strange birds with huge wings and harsh cries. It was covered with dense forest, and near the sea there were quicksands that sucked beasts down to their doom. The mountains of Wales were even higher than they are today, so high that even the eagle could not fly over the mountain tops. And there were bottomless lakes where creatures like huge eels twisted their bodies around the rocks ... creatures with voices that boomed like thunder in the hidden depths.'

'Tell me more,' said Arthur. 'Oh, please tell me more.'

'And then the first men and women landed on these shores,' went on Merlin. 'They came from a faraway land called Troy and they were known as Trojans. They had been defeated in battle by the Greeks and their country laid waste. So they sailed away in search of a land they could turn into a new Troy.'

'And so they landed here!' cried Arthur.

'So they did,' said Merlin, smiling. 'And they called this island Britain, in honour of their leader, Brutus.'

Arthur never tired of hearing this story.

The Angry Knight

One day Arthur was out riding on his own through the forest when he saw an old man a long way ahead – so far away, he couldn't see exactly who it was. Then, to his horror, three men jumped out from the bushes and grabbed hold of the old man! 'They're robbers,' said Arthur to himself, 'but they aren't going to get away with it.' So he spurred on his horse and galloped up as fast as he could.

When the men saw him coming, they ran away – they weren't very brave at all. They didn't mind picking on an old man walking on his own, but they didn't want to fight with someone armed with a sword! Of course they didn't know he was King Arthur – they'd have been even more scared then!

To his surprise, Arthur saw that the old man was Merlin – disguised as an ordinary traveller. 'It's a good job I came along when I did,' said Arthur, 'or you'd be dead by now.'

But Merlin only smiled. 'Not I', he replied. 'You are closer to death than I shall ever be.'

Arthur frowned. 'You talk in riddles,' he said. 'What do you mean by that?'

Merlin wouldn't say. But what he meant was that he – Merlin – could always save himself if he wished, because he had magical powers. But Arthur – although he was king – must die one day, like any other man or woman.

Arthur was still thinking about Merlin's words when he suddenly realised he was alone. Merlin was like that – he would appear and disappear without any warning – it was hard to keep track of him. So Arthur rode on through the forest on his own.

Next thing he knew, an angry-looking man was just ahead of him blocking his way through the forest. The man was dressed as a knight, with a suit of armour and a shield and a sword, and he said to King Arthur, 'Stop! No-one passes me without fighting me first. It's a rule I made, and you must obey it like anyone else.' Of course, he didn't know he was talking to the king.

Arthur replied, 'I don't like your rule, and I'm not afraid of you. Come on then, let's fight.' And they rode at each other with their lances – those long pointed sticks I told you about earlier. But they rode so hard, their lances broke on each other's shields! So they jumped down from their horses, and fought each other with their swords. And then something terrible happened – Arthur's sword broke in two!

'I have you beaten now,' said the knight. 'You must give in, or die.'

'I shall never give in, to you or anyone else,' said Arthur.

The knight lifted his sword, and Arthur feared his last moment had come.

But then something strange happened. The sword suddenly dropped from the knight's hand, and the knight sank to the ground.

Arthur looked around – and there was Merlin!

But instead of being pleased, Arthur was very angry. 'You've killed him with your magic,' he said. 'You shouldn't do that, even to save my life. He was very brave – it's not fair!'

Merlin smiled. 'Don't worry,' he said, 'I haven't killed him. He's just asleep – look.' And Arthur saw that the knight was still breathing.

Pellimore struck down by Merlin's magic

'He'll wake up again soon,' said Merlin. 'His name is Sir Pellinore, and he will be one of your bravest followers.'

So Arthur forgave Merlin, and was glad he had appeared just in time to save his life.

The Lady of the Lake

Arthur and Merlin rode on side by side through the forest. Arthur was very quiet, because he was thinking of Pellinore and what adventures they might have together if they were to be friends instead of enemies.

Then Arthur said suddenly, 'I need a new sword – the last one was broken in two in that fight.'

'We are on our way to find you a sword,' said Merlin. 'A very special sword – you could travel the world and find nothing like it.'

At last they came to a lake. It was right in the middle of the forest and Arthur had never seen it before.

The lake was very beautiful. A gentle breeze touched the waters softly, like a mother's hand, and it was so peaceful that you felt it had been exactly like this since time began.

Arthur looked at the lake, and was filled with wonder. Then Merlin touched his arm. 'Look,' he whispered.

Far out in the lake, an arm clothed in white silk was raised above the water, clutching a sword in its hand. The sword glittered in the sunlight.

'That's the sword I was telling you about,' said Merlin. 'There is nothing like it in the whole wide world.'

'I can well believe it,' said Arthur. For the handle of the sword was covered in jewels.

Just then a boat appeared, with a lady in it. 'Who is that?' asked Arthur, for he was struck by her beauty.

Excaliber

'That's the Lady of the Lake,' said Merlin. 'She lives inside a rock in the lake.'

'How can anyone live inside a rock?' asked Arthur. 'There wouldn't be room!'

'This is a magic rock,' said Merlin. 'If you stepped inside you would enter a strange country. You could travel the world and not find anywhere more beautiful.'

While Arthur was still thinking about this, Merlin said, 'Why don't you try talking to her? You may find she'll give you that sword you can see in the hand reaching above the water.'

The boat came to the shore, and the Lady of the Lake stepped out. Arthur bowed low to her and said, 'My lady, can you tell me something about that sword out there in the lake? Whose is it? How I wish it were mine, for I broke my own sword in battle this very morning.'

'The sword is mine, King Arthur,' she replied, 'but I give it to you gladly. Come, row to where you see the hand holding the sword, and take the sword and its scabbard.'

So Arthur rowed out and took the sword, and as soon as he did so the arm clothed in white silk disappeared under the waters. Arthur rowed back to shore.

He stepped out of the boat and looked at the sword. Its name was carved on the blade – Excaliber. On one side were the words, 'Take me,' and on the other, 'Cast me away.'

'Which do you like better,' asked Merlin, 'the sword

itself or the scabbard it goes in when no-one is using it?'

'The sword, of course,' said Arthur. 'How can there be any doubt?'

Merlin smiled. 'I thought you'd say that,' he said, 'but the fact is that although Excaliber is the finest sword in the whole world, the scabbard will be more use to you in the end – in fact, it will be worth ten swords!'

'Why is that?' asked Arthur wonderingly.

'Because so long as you wear the scabbard, you will lose no blood however badly you are wounded,' said Merlin. 'So remember, always have the scabbard with you when you are likely to run into danger.'

As they rode back through the forest, Arthur thought about all that had happened that day. And that night as he slept, he dreamed about silken arms and shining swords and brave knights sitting around a huge table.

Crowned at Caerleon

Caerleon Castle

Everyone who becomes king or queen has a coronation. That's the day a crown is placed on the sovereign's head, to show that he or she is the rightful ruler of the country.

Today the King or Queen of Britain is crowned in London, but it wasn't always so. King Arthur was crowned in Wales, at a place called Caerleon. Many people will be surprised to hear this, because these days Caerleon isn't at all important. It's just a small town in Gwent, four miles from Newport. But things were very different in the time of King Arthur. If you had gone there then, you would have seen palaces with golden roofs and boats sailing up the River Usk with princes and kings from foreign countries aboard. So you see, it was very important indeed!

The reason for this is that a few hundred years before

Arthur was born, the Romans had built a huge fortress there and called it Isca Silurum. Their buildings were so strong that parts of them are still standing today, after 2,000 years! It was they who had built those palaces with golden roofs in Caerleon. No wonder Arthur wanted to be crowned there!

Now, close your eyes and try to imagine Caerleon as it used to be. The sun comes out and you can't look at the golden roofs – they're too dazzling. On the banks of the river there are houses with lovely gardens. People walk around wearing clothes which look very strange to our eyes. The ladies have long dresses and tall pointed hats, and the men wear short belted tunics covered with highly-coloured robes.

What a day it was, when Arthur was crowned at Caerleon! There were dukes and earls and barons, all looking very proud and important, and princes and princesses from far-away countries. Merchants who made lots of money buying and selling things were there as well, looking around with hungry eyes. You felt they would buy those roofs made out of gold, given half a chance! But not only rich people came. Poor people walked miles and miles to be there, trudging along the dusty roads and trying not to notice how tired they were. Their children held their hands tightly and looked around in wonder at sights they had never seen before. When they reached the town at last, they found it full of noise and excitement. The streets were full of stalls with all sorts of goods on display, and the stallholders did their best to make people buy them. If you have

Arthur's Coronation

been to a street market yourself, you can imagine what it was like!

Now, I'll tell you something I haven't told you before. By this time, Arthur was married and his wife was called Guenevere. People said she was the loveliest lady in the land, but Arthur had not married her just for her beauty. You had only to look into her eyes to see how kind she was. They seemed to reflect the gentleness of her soul, for she was the kind of person who treats people according to their merits, whether they be rich or poor. That went for Arthur, too. He believed in treating his subjects fairly, and they respected him for it. That is why his fame spread far and wide, for there were many bad kings around who had their favourites and didn't care tuppence about the rest.

Guenevere's father was the lord of Camelot. No-one knows now exactly where Camelot was – it may even have been Caerleon itself. Anyway, Guenevere's parents attended the coronation – and how proud they were of their daughter! At her wedding she had worn a gown of green and gold stretching right down to her feet, but they knew she would look lovelier than ever this day, in a dress of pure white.

King Arthur was crowned in a church filled with flowers. Beside him sat Queen Guenevere – everyone thought she must be the loveliest queen who had ever lived. The service did not last long, because King Arthur did not like a lot of fuss – and when they stepped outside the church afterwards, there was such excitement!

King Arthur and Queen Guenevere made their way to a big field, where a feast had been prepared. There were long tables with snow-white cloths on them, and when the King and Queen sat down with the dukes and barons and bishops, the servants brought in food on silver dishes – it made your mouth water just to look at it!

Afterwards there was a tournament – a contest between knights riding on horseback – we heard about this sort of thing earlier, remember? Arthur's knights were such skilful horsemen, everyone stood and watched them. They charged each other in a 'pretend' battle, but took care not to hurt each other too badly. Sometimes, though, they could not avoid knocking one another off their horses with their lances. Of course, their suits of armour protected them, but all the same these tournaments were dangerous – far more dangerous than even the toughest sports you can think of today.

Remember, King Arthur and his knights lived long ago. The hills and mountains of Wales were much the same shape as today, but the valleys and low-lying land were quite different. There were forests far larger than any you would find now, and marshes stretching as far as the eye could see. People had much the same kind of feelings as they have today, but in some ways they had quite a different view of the world. Since they were without cars or trains, even a journey of 10 or 20 miles was an adventure. They were suspicious of strangers, and only the boldest and most trusting of people felt

34

inclined to invite someone they did not know into their homes.

Now, the lord of Camelot – Guenevere's father – wanted to give King Arthur a surprise. So when the tournament was over he said, 'Please follow me, sire.' He led him to a grassy space where a huge round table stood, just like the one Arthur had seen in his dreams. It was so big that 150 knights could sit around it. 'The reason it is round, sire,' said Guenevere's father, 'is that I know all men are equal in your sight. Sitting at this table, no man can say that he is nearer the top of the table than someone else. And you will be chief among your knights simply by virtue of the respect they have for you.'

Arthur replied, 'You have spoken truly, and this table shall be a sign of all that I stand for. I shall choose knights who strive to create a kingdom in which all men and women are treated with justice. The rich people will not be more important than the poor. My knights will be true and honest, and if they hear of a wrong they will try to put it right. When we are all together we will sit at this table, and my knights will be called The Knights of the Round Table.'

Hearing this, everyone cheered.

One of Arthur's knights was called Sir Lancelot du Lac, which means Sir Lancelot of the Lake. He was given this name because when he was a baby, he was taken away by the Lady of the Lake – the very same lady who gave Arthur the sword called Excaliber. Of course, it was wrong of her to steal the child, but she treated him well and brought him up as her own son.

Sir Lancelot was the most famous Knight of the Round Table. Then there was Sir Pellinore, who had begun by fighting Arthur in the forest. Sir Kay, Arthur's

Lancelot du Lac

brother, was a Knight of the Round Table, and so was Sir Tristram. He was a fine harpist, Sir Tristram. He played the harp so sweetly that people said he could charm the birds out of the trees. But the finest harpist in the land was Taliesin, who was also a poet. He lived near Aberystwyth, on the west coast of Wales, and when he was a mere boy he wrote poetry that stirred people to the depths of their souls.

King Arthur loved music and poetry. He was not only a man of action, he was a man of learning. People said he was the wisest king who had ever lived, and I think they were right.

But of course, he could never be as wise as Merlin.

A Wicked Plot

The rule of King Arthur was a golden age in the story of Britain. Never before had there been a king who was so brave and so good. Even bad people tried to live better lives.

Morgan le Fay

But now I am going to tell you something that will surprise you. One of the most evil people of all was Arthur's own sister! She was so wicked she even tried to kill him.

This is how it happened . . .

Arthur's sister was called Morgan le Fay. She was older

than him – and she was very jealous of Arthur. Even Arthur never suspected this, because she disguised it so well. She pretended to like him, and went around saying how wonderful he was, but all the time she hated him and couldn't wait to get rid of him.

Morgan was married to Lord Uriens, but she was secretly in love with a handsome knight called Sir Accolon. In the depths of the night, when everyone was asleep, she lay awake scheming. But in the morning she smiled at her husband as if she had never had a bad thought in her life.

The more she stayed awake like this in the middle of the night, the more twisted she became. She grew pale and thin, but still her husband never suspected anything was wrong. He loved her so much he would never dream of thinking anything bad of her.

The trouble is, Sir Accolon loved her too. He knew he shouldn't because she was married to Lord Uriens, but even the best of men have been known to fall in love with the wrong woman.

What Accolon didn't know is that Morgan meant to kill both her husband and King Arthur, so she could marry Accolon and rule the country with him. He would be King Accolon and she would be Queen Morgan!

I promise you, Sir Accolon had no idea of this evil plan.

One day Arthur and Accolon rode out into the forest

together to hunt stags. By the afternoon they were very tired, and they suddenly realised they were lost. Everything looked strange, and they had no idea which way to go.

'I can't understand it,' said Arthur. 'I thought I knew this forest inside out.'

What he didn't know is that Morgan had cast a spell over them. Yes, she too had magic powers, which she used not for good but for evil!

As darkness fell, King Arthur and Sir Accolon suddenly came across a lake, its waters shimmering in the moonlight. It was the lake where the upraised arm had held Excaliber, but as he was under Morgan's spell he didn't recognise it.

'I haven't seen this lake before,' said King Arthur. 'Have you?'

'No, never,' answered Accolon.

Then they heard music, and realised it was coming from a boat floating out in the lake.

It was music such as they had never heard before . . . very beautiful, but very strange.

They wanted to turn away but couldn't.

The boat drew closer to shore. It was lit by flaming torches – like the Olympic torch we have today. And by the light of those torches they could see lovely maidens on the boat, smiling at them.

There was a feast there too, laid out on the deck ready to eat.

Arthur and Accolon were very hungry, and they went on board and ate the feast.

Afterwards they fell asleep. It was all part of the spell Morgan had cast.

When Arthur woke, he found himself bound hand and foot in chains in a dungeon. When his eyes grew used to the darkness, he saw there were other men around him, all in chains like himself.

'We are prisoners of Sir Damas,' said one of them.

'Where is Sir Accolon?' asked King Arthur. But nobody answered.

At last a maiden appeared. 'I have a message from Sir Damas,' she said. 'Whoever fights and kills his enemy for him will be set free!'

'Unloose me,' cried Arthur. 'I shall do it.'

So they released him from his chains and took him out of the dungeon. They gave him a suit of armour, a helmet and a sword which they told him was his own sword, Excaliber.

He took the sword in his hand and pulled down the visor of his helmet.

Then they led him to the place where he was to fight.

The battle was long and hard. Neither man could see who he was fighting because their faces were covered, except for their eyes.

First Arthur was on top, then his opponent.

'Who are you?' wondered Arthur. 'You are indeed a worthy opponent.'

Just as Arthur thought he had victory within his grasp, his sword snapped!

His opponent raised his sword to strike the mortal blow.

Then the sword fell from his hand. Arthur turned to see the Lady of the Lake standing there.

He flung his useless sword down and picked up his opponent's. To his astonishment, he found *this* sword was Excaliber – he had been fighting with the wrong weapon!

He was so angry that he struck his opponent with Excaliber. Blood gushed from the wound.

'Kill me!' cried the man in agony.

Arthur froze. It was Sir Accolon's voice!

He raised the man's visor and saw it really was Accolon.

Arthur was filled with horror, to think that he had fought one of his dearest friends to the death. And of course, Accolon had not known he was fighting Arthur.

All this had happened because of Morgan le Fay's treachery. It was she who had placed Excaliber in Accolon's hand, telling him he would be fighting an unknown knight for her. She was sure he was bound to win, with Excaliber. And he would have triumphed too, if the Lady of the Lake had not come to Arthur's rescue. It was her magic power that had saved him.

Arthur killing Accolon

When Arthur found out what his sister had done, he realised for the first time how evil she was. Full of anger, he sent Sir Accolon's body to her. How she wept to see her lover dead, and her wicked plan defeated!

But this isn't the end of the story. For Morgan, fearing what Arthur might do now he had found her out, decided to rob him of his most deadly weapon, Excaliber. So right away, she went to the place where he had been taken to rest after his duel with Accolon. He was being cared for by nuns, who told her he was sleeping and should not be disturbed. 'Take me to him,' she demanded angrily. 'He is my brother – you cannot keep me from him.'

They were afraid of her, so showed her to the room where Arthur lay sleeping.

When she was alone with him, she tip-toed to the bed. In his right hand he clutched Excaliber – clutched it so tightly, even in his sleep, that she knew she could not take it from him without waking him up. So she took the scabbard and rode away.

When Arthur awoke and found the scabbard gone, he was very angry. For remember, the Lady of the Lake had told him never to be without the scabbard, which was worth more to him than ten swords.

'Who has been here?' he asked the nuns.

'Your sister,' they replied.

'You shouldn't have let her in,' he cried. 'You have betrayed my faith in you.' And he saddled his horse and rode off in pursuit of her, with Sir Ontzlake riding beside him.

Their horses were very swift, and at last they caught sight of her in the distance. They spurred their horses on, and rode even faster.

When she saw how they were gaining on her, she flung the scabbard into a lake, and there it was lost for ever.

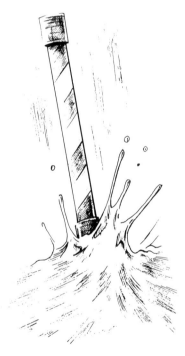

Scabbard falling

So now Arthur lacked its protection, and could be killed in battle like anyone else.

And Morgan? Well, she was so scared now that she went to live far away in a huge castle set on a high rock. She was so frightened that she only showed her face outside its thick walls at night. But the story of how she had tried to kill Arthur went around the kingdom, and nobody had a good word to say for her any more.

The Quest for the Grail

King Arthur was true to his word. His knights went around the country righting wrongs and making sure that rich and powerful people did not treat poor people badly.

Remember, in those days the rich often lived in big castles full of servants and soldiers, while the poor had to be content with miserable little huts made out of branches and twigs, with clay to fill in the gaps. Even the rich people, though, did not possess some of the things we take for granted. There were very few books, and of course no radio or television, and they could not even have a cup of tea or coffee because such things had not yet been brought to this country. What is more, their castles were very cold in winter because they were draughty and it was impossible to heat them properly. They kept coal and wood fires burning day and night, but you were only really warm if you were close to the fire.

What the rich and the poor had in common was their religion, for they were all Christians. They made a special point of going to church every Easter Day, when we remember how Jesus rose from the dead after being crucified, and naturally they knew all about the Last Supper he had with his disciples.

It's the Last Supper that comes into this story of King Arthur.

We call it the Last Supper because it was the very last

Last supper

meal that Jesus had with his twelve closest friends, whom we call the disciples. They met in an upstairs room and ate bread and drank wine. They drank the wine from a large cup which came to be known as the Holy Grail. After Jesus had gone to Heaven, his followers looked after this cup because it reminded them of Him. First one of them took care of it, then another. But there came a time when few people knew exactly where it was.

One day King Arthur and his knights were seated at the Round Table in Camelot when they heard a very loud clap of thunder. Then a bright light filled the room, as if sunlight were pouring through the ceiling. They were startled and a bit frightened – it was so weird and unexpected. The strangest thing of all was, everyone thought the others looked different somehow – it wasn't simply that the light was so bright, but that it seemed to make all the good things inside them show up in their faces.

Then the Holy Grail was carried into the room. It was covered with white silk, so they couldn't actually see it – but all the same, for some reason they all seemed to know exactly what it was. And suddenly everything seemed perfect – there was the smell of spring flowers in the air, and they all felt they could have everything in the world they had ever wanted.

This feeling, however, was not to last, because suddenly the Grail disappeared. They couldn't tell how or where it went – one moment it was there, and the next it had vanished!

The Knights of the Round Table, who had been dumbstruck by these happenings, found their tongues once more.

'Where has it gone?' they said. 'What does it all mean?'

And they were saddened to find that the smell of spring flowers was fading.

King Arthur stood up. 'We must thank the Lord Jesus,' he said, 'for showing this miracle to us.'

And one of his knights, Sir Gawain, said: 'It was truly a marvellous sight. My only regret is that we didn't actually see the Holy Grail, because it was covered by the white silk cloth. I now make a vow, that I shall search far and wide for the Grail, and not return to this court till I have seen it with my own eyes.'

Then one of the other knights stood up and said, 'I'll do the same!' So did a third knight, then a fourth, until nearly all the Knights of the Round Table had made a solemn promise to travel the world in search of the Grail.

This became known as The Quest – or Search – for the Grail.

Then suddenly they realised how sad King Arthur was looking.

'Oh, Gawain,' he said with a sigh, 'you can't imagine how miserable you've made me. For it means you'll all be going away, and leaving me here. We'll never be together again as we are now, because some of you are sure to die in your quest for the Grail.'

Sir Lancelot said, 'If we do die, Sire, it surely won't be as bad as you think. We all have to die some day, and to die while searching for the Grail would be an honour.'

King Arthur looked at him. 'Ah, Lancelot,' he said, 'never has any king in the whole world had such good men with him as I've had this day at the Round Table. That's why I feel sad, because we are going our separate ways, and it means the end of our old comradeship.'

And nobody knew what to say.

When Queen Guenevere found out what was happening, she too was sad, and so were the ladies of the court.

'Why is my husband letting them do this?' asked the Queen. But in her heart, she knew why. For the King would never try to persuade anyone to break a promise.

So the Knights of the Round Table rode out of Camelot, and King Arthur was so sad that he shut himself in a room all on his own.

And Queen Guenevere wept. And so did the ladies of the court.

The knights met with many adventures on their travels. They journeyed through strange lands, and saw some amazing sights. They crossed wide oceans, sailed along rivers, and went to the help of people in trouble. And at last Sir Lancelot came to a sea called Mortaise. There he lay down on the shore and slept. And in his dream he heard a voice say, 'Sir Lancelot, arise, and go on board the first ship you see.' He woke up at once, and walked along the shore, and soon he came to a ship without any sails. As soon as he stepped aboard he felt very peaceful and happy – much the same as he had felt when the Holy Grail had appeared.

Who can blame him for staying there awhile? And then he had a surprise. For one day, as he was out walking, who should he see but one of the other Knights of the Round Table – Sir Galahad. They were overjoyed, for they had missed one another, and all their other comrades.

'Let's stay together,' said Lancelot, 'and continue our search for the Holy Grail!'

Galahad agreed at once, so they set off together. But then there came a day when a knight on a white horse appeared before them, and this knight told Galahad he must go the rest of the way on his own. So he said goodbye to Lancelot, and continued his journey alone.

At last he came to a mighty castle called Carbonek,

Gallahad – searching for the grail

and there he found two other Knights of the Round Table, Sir Percival and Sir Bors.

'I've had such adventures!' said Bors. 'I've been through dark forests and to the tops of high mountains – it's a year and a half since I've been anywhere near a town or village.'

'I've had adventures too,' said Galahad. 'And by the shores of a sea I met Lancelot. We stayed together for a long time, and fought wild beasts in the jungle.' Then Percival told them stories he had heard on his journey – stories of Merlin the magician, who had prophesied that the Holy Grail would be seen only by Knights of the Round Table.

So Galahad and Bors and Percival went into the castle together.

They passed through one heavy iron door after another, and were amazed that nobody tried to stop them – it was as though they were expected. And at last they found the Holy Grail – the cup that Jesus had held

Gallahad kneeling before the grail

in His hands at the Last Supper. It was on a silver table, and four angels stood around it.

They knelt before the Grail, and said a prayer of thankfulness.

Arthur and the Sleeping Knights

When King Arthur heard how three of his knights had seen the Holy Grail, he was very proud of them. But he was sad as well, because only half the Knights of the Round Table returned home from the Quest. Some were taken ill and died in faraway countries, while others were killed by wild animals.

What made him even sadder is that his kingdom was being torn apart by violent quarrels. Many of the rich lords were fighting one another, and there were even those who envied Arthur his crown and wanted to be king in his place.

Strange as it may seem, some of the most jealous people were to be found in Arthur's own family. They were his five nephews, Gawain, Gaheris, Agravaine, Gareth and Mordred, who lived on the isle of Orkney in Scotland.

These brothers hated Lancelot, because he was King Arthur's favourite knight. 'It's not fair,' they grumbled. 'It's only because Lancelot's the favourite that he's been raised up so high in the court. King Arthur's our uncle – why doesn't he take more notice of us?'

One day Agravaine could stand it no longer. He called his brothers together and said, 'I think Lancelot wants to be king himself! I'm going to see King Arthur at once and warn him.'

His eldest brother, Gawain, didn't like this at all. 'I don't think that's true for a moment,' he said. 'If you spread that rumour, there's sure to be war between Lancelot and ourselves. Remember, Lancelot's very popular – most people will side with him, not with us. What's more, Lancelot saved my life once. And he saved yours too, Agravaine, and yours, Mordred!'

'I don't care,' said Agravaine. 'I'm going to tell the King just the same.' And that's what he did.

King Arthur said, 'I don't believe you. Lancelot isn't just my best knight, he's my best friend too. He would never plot against me like that!'

'I'm sorry, Sire,' said Agravaine, 'but what I say is true, and I can prove it. If you go out hunting tomorrow, you'll find that Lancelot will stay behind with the Queen. And while you're out, they'll be plotting against you.'

So the King went hunting next day, and Lancelot did stay behind. And later that day, he was found alone with the Queen. But he was with her only because he was so fond of her, not because he wanted to be King.

Of course, Arthur couldn't be sure of this. When he was told that Lancelot and the Queen really had been found alone together when he was out hunting, he thought: 'Perhaps the story's true after all. Maybe Lancelot *does* want to be King instead of me.'

And he knew that he could never again trust Lancelot as he had before.

Then a civil war broke out in King Arthur's kingdom. Some sided with Lancelot, and others with the King. The fighting went on a long time before a truce was called and Arthur said, 'I want to hold a meeting with Lancelot to try to patch up this quarrel. We shouldn't be fighting each other like this.'

And Lancelot agreed. 'I have no real quarrel with King Arthur,' he said. 'It's only because people spread rumours about me that we started fighting in the first place.'

So a meeting was arranged between King Arthur and Lancelot.

They met at Caerleon – the very place where the brotherhood of the Round Table had begun, so many years before. King Arthur and Lancelot looked sadly at one another, and they both knew in their hearts that although they didn't want to go on fighting each other, so many bad things had happened that they could never again be such close friends as they had been before.

'I shall leave Britain,' said Lancelot, 'and go to live in France. But I want you to know, Sire, that I was proud to be a Knight of the Round Table, and I think it's a great shame that our old comradeship should have ended like this.'

As Lancelot spoke these words, Queen Guenevere stood quietly by King Arthur's side. Only once did she raise her eyes, and that was when Lancelot said goodbye. She and Lancelot exchanged a glance, and then he was gone.

When the door closed behind him, the King knew that never again would his knights sit at the Round Table.

But I'm sorry to say that this wasn't the end of all the fighting. For now Arthur's nephew Mordred tried to seize his throne. Some sided with him and others with King Arthur. The fighting went on for ages – it seemed it would never end.

Lancelot and Guinevere

Then one night Arthur dreamt that Gawain came to warn him that if he fought Mordred next day, he would be killed in battle – and so would Mordred.

'Put off the battle for a month,' said Gawain in the dream, 'and in that time Lancelot will come back from France, and join forces with you to beat Mordred.'

The dream was so vivid that Arthur saw it as a warning. When Arthur woke up he said, 'I can't fight Mordred today!' And he explained why.

So King Arthur and Mordred met to sign a peace treaty saying the war was over. But just then an adder crawled out of a bush and bit a knight in the foot. Now an adder is a snake with a poisonous bite, so the knight drew his sword to kill it.

The trouble is, no-one saw the snake – all they saw was the man drawing his sword. And they were so suspicious of each other, they thought he was going to kill someone. So they all began fighting again.

King Arthur was so angry that he rushed at Mordred with his sword, Excaliber, and thrust it deep into Mordred's body. Mordred knew he was mortally wounded, but with one last effort he took his sword in both hands and lunged at Arthur. So great was the blow that his sword pierc-ed the King's helmet, and entered his brain.

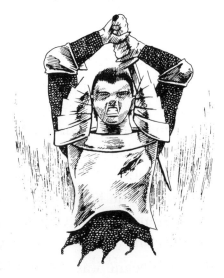

People rushed to Arthur's side, but there was little they could do. Within a few hours he was dead.

Some say Arthur was carried away on a barge to a ghostly land called the Vale of Avalon. But others believe this last battle was fought in Wales, near Beddgelert in

Mordred about to slay Arthur .

Gwynedd, and that after being wounded Arthur was carried to a cave in the mountains. There he and his knights still lie to this day – not dead, but sleeping.

The story goes that one day, when Wales needs them, they will awake!

And where exactly is this cave? Ah, if we knew that we would be as wise as Merlin – for only Merlin knows. But I can tell you this much. One day, about 100 years ago, a shepherd came across it by accident. Stepping into the cave, he brushed against something and a loud bell rang out. The knights began to wake up and the shepherd ran away, leaving the knights to drift back into sleep once more.

Another time, a man carrying a hazel stick was going to Bala Fair when someone stopped him and said he was sure there was buried treasure by the tree from which the stick had been cut. They hurried to the spot and came across the cave. Full of curiosity, they stepped inside – but the bell rang out again and the knights woke up saying, 'Has the day come?'

'No!' cried the men in terror, not really knowing what the knights meant by saying this – and you never saw anyone run so fast as those two men, out of the cave and down the mountain.

So there they remain to this day, King Arthur and his knights, waiting . . . waiting . . . waiting for the call that will say Wales needs them once more.

And that is why Arthur is called the Once . . . And *Future* King.

Shepherd and sleeping knights

And Merlin? He isn't asleep, but very much awake. You can't see him, but you can feel his presence with you as you go around Wales. Not all the time . . . but when you are up in the hills with the wind blowing through your hair and you are filled with wonder at the beauty of it all, that's Merlin whispering to you.

When you are walking the sands and the sea seems to be trying to tell you something, that's Merlin.

When you hear Welsh voices uplifted in song and you catch your breath, that's Merlin giving you a hint of the wonder of Wales.

And as the sun plunges into the shimmering sea, it is Merlin who paints the sky a myriad colours.

Merlin is the spirit of Wales . . . a spirit generous to those who seek to understand her, and who sense her ageless magic.

ALSO AVAILABLE FROM JOHN JONES PUBLISHING LTD

FEET IN CHAINS by Kate Roberts. Translated from the Welsh by John Idris Jones. "Her characters are motivated by the need to survive poverty with some dignity, independence and self-respect. She is skilful at her craft, welding her short chapters into a strong bridge to link the generations and decades she writes about." *Tribune* "I urge it strongly for its distillation of time and place and people . . . triumphantly alive in their own small corner." *The Guardian* "A seminal work of Welsh-language fiction and one which has drawn praise from critics, not only in Wales but in England and America. It remains one of the finest novels which I have read by any writer." Dewi Roberts *Cambrensis* 1996 "It is a mark of the compelling power of this short novel and the vitality of its translation by John Idris Jones that it seems important we should know what Kate Roberts was really saying . . . we admire the force of this narrative . . ." Richard Jones *The New Welsh Review* Autumn 1996.

ISBN 1 871083 80 X   Price £4.99

TEA IN THE HEATHER by Kate Roberts. Translated by Wyn Griffith. Eight stories set in Caernarfonshire in the early years of the twentieth century. They are clear, historically accurate accounts of the lives of smallholding hill farmers and quarrymen, holding their culture together in the face of deprivation. There is a central link in the presence of the girl Begw; the first story presents her at the age of about three; in the last one she is nine. Her friend Winni is a rebel, old before her time. These are moving, unforgettable stories. With a new Preface by Derec Llwyd Morgan.

ISBN 1 871083 85 0   Price £4.99